Who can believe in witches?

and other stories

This is a work of fiction. Names, characters, businesses, places, events, locales, and incidents are either the products of the author's imagination or used in a fictitious manner.

First published in the UK in 2023 by Holborn House Ltd.

©2023 Cheryl Burman

Apart from any use permitted under UK copyright law, this publication may only be reproduced, stored, or transmitted, in any form, or by any means, with the prior permission in writing of the publishers or, in the case of reprographic production, in accordance with the terms and licences issued by the Copyright Licensing Agency.

NOVELS

Keepers

Book two *Walking in the Rain:* a novella

Book three *The Past can Wait:* a novella

River Witch

COLLECTED SHORT STORIES

Dragon Gift: ten short stories

Who can believe in witches? and other stories

GUARDIANS OF THE FOREST

Book one *The Wild Army*

Book two *Quests*

Book three *Gryphon Magic*

Prequel *Legend of the Winged Lion*

Sequel *Winter of the White Horde*

https://cherylburman.com/books/

Contents

Who can believe in witches
in the year of our Lord 1906? 7

No hodding 22

Sabrina rising 36

The making of a wise woman 42

St Ceyna whispers 56

Five days, five nights 65

Orchard kingdom. 69

The death of the Loch Ard 72

Carriers of grief 76

The clarity of sun on water 80

Guy Fawkes, guy, 'twas his intent
to blow up king and parliament. 86

Peacock kite 89

Acknowledgements 91

Introduction

My first collection of short stories, published in 2021, took on a mythical, fairytale theme. I'd had some success with flash fiction pieces in the fantasy and magical realism styles, and it seemed a good idea to put them into one place and send them into the wild. Thus *Dragon Gift* was born, with most of its readership comprising new signups to my newsletter during 2021 to the end of 2023.

Who can believe in witches? is a different kind of collection. All the stories, bar one, are based on historical happenings and/or people. The exception is Peacock kite, purely imaginative but set – in my mind at least – in the late 19th century.

While my first novels were fantasy for young people (with a strong much older fan base), my books for grownups have historical settings and are loosely based on or inspired by real people. Of course, that doesn't stop me introducing a hint of fantasy, as in *River Witch*, and in these stories you will find two or three veering in that direction.

Most of these tales are Forest of Dean based. Over the years I've lived here I have mined a little of the rich vein of history and tradition in which the Forest is steeped. I intend to keep doing so.

Enjoy these stories, and do let me know you have by leaving a review, or even a rating, on Amazon or Goodreads. Thank you!

Cheryl
December 2023

Cheryl Burman

Forest inspired

Who can believe in witches in the year of our Lord 1906?

Shortlisted in the Historical Writers' Association 2023 Dorothy Dunnett Short Story Competition, this tale is based on the true story of Ellen Hayward from Cinderford in the Forest of Dean, tried for witchcraft in 1906.

Here are the judges' comment on the story:

"…this story explores the persecution of women, especially those who did not conform to convention: unwedded mothers, healers and wise women, and those blamed for the actions of lustful men. A dual timeline is no easy feat within a short story but Cheryl Burman pulls it off, leading to a satisfying conclusion."

'YOU KNOW HOW THEY FOUND her?'

Sergeant Cooper is smug above his thick, dark moustache. Ellen doesn't know, only that however they found her, it will bode her, Ellen, no good. She gazes out the parlour window to the rows of herb pots blossoming in the May warmth and the tidy beds where flowers will soon spill their health-giving profusion.

'Wandering through the trees, she was.' Cooper leans towards Ellen, his voice a heavy buzz in her ear. 'Three days and nights she been in there, lost.'

Ellen faces him, her expression neutral. Cooper is not the first fool she has suffered.

'Hair tangled with leaves and grass, skirts torn.' He leers. 'Could see her bloomers, filthy as they was.'

'Poor soul,' Ellen murmurs.

'Ha! You might say so, given she was waving a hazel stick, calling out about keeping the witches away.' His button black eyes corrode only the back of Ellen's head, for she has returned to her inspection of the garden.

Yes, this is what he has come for. Markey has been loud in his accusations of witchcraft. Who has my stolen money? he demanded. A simple enough question for such as Ellen. She bade him peer into a crystal, the man tells all who will listen (there are many), revealing therein secrets he would not have learned, scandalous secrets. Afterwards, a madness not of this world struck down his daughter, his granddaughter. They languish in the asylum. Now his wife will join them.

Ellen keeps her gaze neutral. She will not help Cooper with denials or statements of innocence. He can torture it from her, as they have ever done with those accused. Cooper, with his judgemental morality, would have fitted well with the past. Ellen envisions him in a coned witchfinder's hat, cloak flying behind like crow's wings as he leads the excited procession to the dunking pond, or the hanging tree. She shuts the images away. There will be no dunking, no hanging. There will be shame, humiliation, and the death of a hard-earned livelihood.

Sensing trouble – or scandal, depending on their natures – neighbours have gathered. They shuffle their feet on the cracked paved path from the front door to the iron gate, and beyond onto the dirt road. They whisper, point, scowl.

'All your doing, Mother Hayward,' Cooper jeers. 'Which is why you're coming with me, charged all proper.' He unfolds a piece of paper and reads aloud, with particular enjoyment of certain words: 'unlawfully', 'pretended witchcraft', 'deceive'.

Ellen lifts her chin, asks, 'Who will feed my hens?'

'They'll be fed.' The policeman uses his dusty boot to push a white bird across the bare floor boards. It cackles, lifts its wings in protest. 'Or become food.' He smirks.

Ellen turns from his smugness, seeking a sympathetic eye among the crowd which has now seeped into the parlour itself. Granny Kear gives a slight nod and the hens are off the list of Ellen's worries. Outside, the flowers and massed pots will survive the season's gentle, damp warmth. She need not concern herself over hens and plants. Much else remains.

She squints at the policeman through eyes grown weak with age and too much close work. 'I'm no witch, Sergeant Cooper,' she says. 'Who can believe in witches in the year of our Lord, 1906?'

Cooper snorts. 'We'll let the magistrate decide that. And don't you be taking our Lord's name in vain, else it'll go worse for you.' He grips her elbow. 'Get your coat.'

The neighbours shuffle awkwardly in the constraints of the hallway. Room is made for Ellen and her uniformed escort.

Cooper is forced to stop when Granny Kear steps forward, presses Ellen's shoulder with arthritically knobbled fingers. 'Don't thee fret, Ellen, it'll come out all right.'

'More witches, a whole coven likely,' Cooper mumbles.

Granny Kear ignores his glare and steps aside.

...

The cold of the cell's flagstones leaches through Ellen's thin soles. She wraps her shawl about her shoulders and sits on the cot. There is one blanket, no pillow, but Ellen has never rested her head on a pillow, a luxury for better-off folk than she's ever been. The evening darkens through the high, barred window. This place where they hold her is not far from her old haunt, the workhouse. Not that any here will learn that from her. Twenty-five years ago.

Busy with the townsfolk's ailments and life's everyday problems, Ellen's chances for reflection are few, though greater in number than the times she wishes to reflect. Now her mind insists, because if Granny Kear is wrong, the workhouse is where Ellen will end her days. The straw mattress crackles beneath the sudden trembling of her slim weight.

'Hey, you, are you the witch?'

The question is tossed across the gap between the rows of cells. Ellen ignores it.

'Cast a spell on 'em all, sent 'em mad!'

Shocked intakes of breaths, broken by giggles.

'They burn witches, don't they?' Laughter.

'Where's the cat?' Shrieked amusement.

Others take up the calls, their heckling merging into one strident screech to assail Ellen's ears. Her pulse thumps.

A thug in uniform paces down the barely lit passageway, battering a truncheon against bars – and fingers clenched to the bars, if too slow to be removed – boosting the din with his shouts of shut up you poxy whores.

Ellen remains on the cot, her hands in their half-mittens clenched beneath her bony buttocks.

Whore.

The word rattles in her tired, frightened brain.

It's the same word hissed many years ago in Ellen's face by her sour-faced sister-in-law. Her brother stood by, arms dangling, useless when not at his fishing.

Whore.

Ellen is back in the tiny room with its bed as narrow as the gaol cot, a scratched chest for her clothes the only other furniture. Her sister-in-law spat out her righteousness.

'We took you in, gave you a home, let you make a respectable living. Look how you repay us.'

The baby, pinkly new, squalled his hunger.

The gaol heckles fall away, the prisoners retreat into the dark places of their cells. There are whispers, cackles – forced or otherwise. Minutes pass. The air chills. An hour, perhaps. Snores, coughs, snuffles assault the silence. They are feeble, ineffectual against Ellen's spinning mind.

She shifts on the mattress, lies on her side to face the stone wall, and eases her stiff legs onto the cot. She keeps her boots on. Her heart beats with emotions she didn't know she still possessed. They don't belong with the calm, respectable, widowed Mrs Ellen Hayward, sought after wise woman and herbalist.

For over twenty years, people have trotted out their petty problems, laid them before her to deal with. Rashes, persistent headaches, a child with a wheezing cough. A lover gone astray or not yet caught. A lost brooch, mislaid money. Or was it stolen? Ellen advises, offers herbs and potions of her own learned and tried concoctions. Old people, mothers, those with the bloom of youth on their cheeks, show their gratitude with plant cuttings, a flitch of bacon, a collar of lace. A hen or two.

So much time has passed. She has dragged herself to respectability. Wide awake, Ellen's mind insists on diving into its well of ancient, stifled memories.

Orphaned, plain, sullen, a resented burden on her brother's family, which only her skilful dressmaking diminished, barely. Until he came, the well-dressed customer with his smooth words and smoother promises. *Come walk with me by the river*, he said, taking her arm and leading her to the clifftop paths where his caresses and summer's breezes gently fanned Ellen's ardour.

My sweet Ellen. He stroked her arms, her neck, pulled her close, drew her down into the green shade of the high bracken where lovers have hidden for centuries. She gave herself, grateful to be desired.

We will marry.

His last words to her, before he left the village with the stealth, and doubtless the complacency, of a satiated tomcat.

Cloaks are a wondrous device for hiding the consequence of illicit love, but no cloak can hide a shameful birth. So there she was, in the bedroom with the wooden chest and an apoplectic sister-in-law, exposed in all senses.

Cast out by her brother and his wife, Ellen walked with head down to the river ferry, her newborn son cradled against her in his makeshift sling. The villagers traced her banishment with condemning gazes. A cloth bag was slung over her shoulder. All for the baby, her own meagre belongings sacrificed to the ease of cheap travel. Those sharing the ferry with her kept their distance, in case her sin should taint them. They huddled at one end like puppies in a box, wishing the cold journey to be over, their minds on warming fires and hot food.

As on the homeward side of the broad river, Ellen had nowhere to lay her and the baby's heads. She wandered up the steep road, past windows where chinks of candlelight gleamed through drawn curtains. The scent of roasting meats tickled her nostrils. She found shelter in the porch of the great church, and the next day used her few pennies to rent a hovel of a cottage.

She squirms on the gaol cot, crackling the straw,

and shudders a breath. Tears not shed for decades prick her eyes. The cottage, more ruin than building. A broken table, a glassless window hung with a hessian sack. A freezing wind gusted through the gap under the door to dampen the already weak warmth of the fire. The baby weakened too. When the men came, they found his cheeks sunken and his cries thin.

...

It's near dawn when sleep captures Ellen, briefly, before banging on the bars shocks her awake. Gruel for breakfast, eaten in silence at a long table with other inmates. They return to their cells.

Ellen has a visitor.

'How long must I be here?' she asks Sergeant Cooper.

'As long as it takes.'

He stands outside her cell, suggesting his visit will be brief. Ellen stays seated on the cot. She wants to ask about the hens, except it would give him pleasure to taunt her. Instead she says, 'How is Mrs Markey?'

Cooper's button eyes gleam. He twists the end of his moustache. 'Not only her what gone mad.'

She will not ask about this either, despite the faster pattering of her heart. Cooper will tell her, he can't help himself.

'The son, George. Neighbour found him in his kitchen, rambling nonsense, neighbour says, about *witchery* being practiced on his family.' He pokes a dirty-nailed finger through the bars, waggles it. 'I wonder who he be thinking of?'

Ellen folds her hands in her lap to hide their trembling.

Some days ago, Markey came to her house, hat

scrunched in his black-nailed fingers, garbling a tale of money, a substantial amount, stolen from his home, from a locked drawer in a locked room.

'Who stole it, Mother Hayward? Find 'em, tell me.' He paced among the hens, muttering about not trusting anyone, not even family.

Cooper's cough interrupts Ellen's thoughts. 'Your old friend Doctor Carlton, it was him sent George to the asylum.' He squints at her, the knowing curve of his full lips peering through the shrubbery of his moustache.

When Ellen keeps her silence, Cooper humphs and turns to leave. 'No silences in court, *Mother* Hayward. We'll hear it all then.' He bows, mocking her, and strides away. His boots clump on the stone flags.

Doctor Carlton. Ellen pulls in her lips, seeing it all again, plain as day.

The doctor strode in to the chilly hovel, no polite knocking. He glanced at the squalling baby, frowned at the freezing, filthy room, and shook his head. He looked questioningly at his companion.

'Workhouse,' the other said. Well fed, this one, with plump red cheeks sprouting a wiry ginger beard.

'No.' Ellen hugged her son closer, as if the mere feel of her breasts might nourish him. 'No, please.'

'You want the babe to die of hunger, exposure?' The doctor peered into the scrunched face.

'We could take the babe, leave you,' the ginger man said. 'Easy enough to find a home for it, once it's been fattened up.' When he poked the baby's chest, Ellen gagged at his sour breath.

'What's it to be?' Doctor Carlton said. His tone was almost kindly.

...

There's a new prisoner for the inmates to gloat over. A skeletal lass, caught for thieving a ribbon. She huddles in a corner, crying. The women either comfort or curse her, depending on their tolerance for noisy fright. For now, they ignore Ellen. There will be ample opportunity to return to her after her trial, if she is convicted.

The workhouse inmates didn't ignore her arrival, the baby adding to the drama. They clustered around, glad of a fresh tale, especially one spiced with immorality. Whispers tracked Ellen's movements by day and hung in the long dormitory's fuggy air at night. Lying on the iron cot with her son folded against her, she closed her ears to salacious gossip.

Watery, lukewarm gruel kept her from starvation, but the baby did not thrive. He refused her derisory offerings and lifted his own curled fist to chew. His eyes were screwed tight, his too-thin face wrinkled like an un-ironed shirt.

'If'n he won't feed, they'll sell him to the baby farmer.' The words were hissed into Ellen's ear from the next bed, less than two handspans away.

An ancient woman with face and throat made of the same stuff as her rumpled brown dress, this one had held back from the accusing glares.

'Baby farmer?' Terror seethed in Ellen's gut. 'No.'

A dry, cackling laugh. 'It's a way to be relieved of the object of your shame, girl. Start over.' The old woman snorted. 'And mebbe the babe will find himself loving parents.'

Ellen shakes in horror. More like he will end as a tiny corpse in a rough-made grave beside a stinking privy.

'No.'

The word soughed across the space and the old woman caught it, returned it with a muttered, 'There be a second way.'

...

Dust motes lit by early morning sunlight through the high window float in the corner of Ellen's cell. She blinks, hauls her stiff bones to a sitting position and eases her legs to the floor. The chill of the flags pierces her stockinged feet, snakes its way up her body to nestle in the pit of her stomach.

Today is the day the magistrate will make his decision.

She forces down breakfast's gruel, gagging. Back in her cell, she asks for water, a cloth and a comb, and is handed them with a shrug. She washes her face, brushes her black skirt with the damp cloth, twists her grey, thin hair into as neat a bun as she can with no benefit of a mirror. She sits on the straw mattress, hands in her lap, and waits.

Like she waited for the crone from the workhouse to whisper what this second way might be. Curled on her side, the woman had reached under her mattress and pulled out a stained calico pouch, bulging with whatever it held.

'Take it,' she hissed. 'I've no more need of it.'

Ellen drew back. 'What is it?'

The turnkey raps the bars of Ellen's cell with his truncheon.

'Time,' he says.

He unlocks the door, beckoning her out. She walks stiff-necked into the passageway, eyes on the man's black-coated back.

Heckling and laughter shadow her short journey to the outer door.

'See you back here soon!'

'Cast spells on 'em all.'

'Fly away.'

There'll be no flying away. Not this time.

...

'Ellen Hayward.'

Ellen startles at her name spoken in the clarion tones of the court clerk. The words of the charges reach her like the distant rumble of thunder over the river. Threatening, impersonal.

'... she did unlawfully use certain craft or means or device, to wit, by pretended witchcraft ...'

She stares ahead as the first witness, Sergeant Cooper, is called, aware that every seat and bench in the high-ceilinged room is crammed to bursting with spectators. Aware too of Cooper's pompous accusations destroying, word by malicious word, the life she has carefully, assiduously created. Her chest tightens. She clutches the railing of the dock to save herself from falling.

There would be a judgement, a reckoning, one day. Ellen has always understood this. Yet over the years the understanding faded like curtains at a too sunny window, until only the barest pattern remains.

The memory of the workhouse plays more clearly in her head than the courthouse scene.

The crone had eased herself half upright, her bony shoulders in their greying nightgown pushed against the iron bedstead. She loosened the drawstring of the pouch, pulled it open and thrust it towards Ellen. The escaping scent writhed in the air, faintly luminous, a living thing, with strength to overcome the fuggy stench of the dormitory. Sharp tang of rosemary, mustiness of rue, and odours Ellen did not recognise. She breathed it in. Her mind swirled, the scent sharpening her senses: the breaths of each inmate, the restlessness of their limbs, their mutterings and fartings.

Ellen's mind is jolted to the present by muffled sniggers from the crowd. Markey is telling his tale. His eyes are wild, his answers bumbling, incoherent. She frowns. The sniggers erupt into untrammelled laughter. The clerk shouts for order. Markey glares at the spectators, at the clerk, at the magistrate. His eyes shift briefly to Ellen, and away again. He is told to return to his seat while others are called.

Others? More like Cooper? Is Ellen to go full circle?

The old woman in the grey nightgown had grinned

a toothless grin. 'Tis a little magic,' she said. 'All is for buying, if you know how to pay.'

'Magic?' Heady, savouring the scents, Ellen shifted her gaze from the pouch to the baby, and back to the leathery face. 'Then why are you in this place, Mother?'

'For you.' The woman coughed, brought her free hand to her scrawny throat. 'Go on, have it.'

Ellen clasped the greasy calico. The crone shifted on the straw mattress, bade Ellen do the same, and touched foreheads across the gap. The murmur of secret words buzzed in Ellen's ears – incomprehensible, yet each one bearing meaning. Each sentence carrying new life. The baby, fretfully asleep in her arms, loosened a tiny fist from his swaddling and waved it. His mouth pursed, seeking food.

The crone's murmurings faded into a blankness broken by the baby bawling his demands in the early dawn. His cries were lusty, his weak mewling a thing of yesterday. Ellen's full breasts tingled, demanding their own satisfaction.

In the next cot, the old woman lay on her back, the blanket pulled to her chin. Her eyes were open, yet whatever she saw, it was not the cobwebbed rafters of the dormitory. Ellen felt for the pouch at her side, tucked it into the baby's blanket. The workhouse inmates, alerted by the mysterious way of these things, gathered around the wizened body. Their eyes were sombre, their lips trembled.

The same sombre eyes are borne by the townsfolk as they come forward to take the witness stand. The stifling, sweat-soaked air is trapped in Ellen's lungs. She grasps the dock railing to counter the tremulous failure of her legs.

Would she undo it? Would she refuse the pouch, the old crone's whispers?

If it pleases his honour, each witness asserts, he should know how Mother Hayward's herbs and potions have cured their coughs and rashes, how her wise counselling has helped solve life's dilemmas, how they respect her, how she does all this willingly, at no charge.

Ellen slides her hand into the deep pocket of her skirt, touches the threadbare pouch, now black with age and long use. Her breath eases with each testament. Her aching fingers loosen their grip, and her legs steady.

The magistrate nods. Mother Hayward is no witch. She has no magic, simply skills and the experiences of a long life.

Ellen lifts her eyes, seeking her son, grown tall, robust. He stands at the back, ensuring she can see him. He tilts his head to the side, grins their secret across the heads of the crowd.

No hodding

8,000 miners in the Forest of Dean were without work from 31 March to 1 July in the 1921 national miners' lockout.

'God's beautiful sunshine' comes from a letter to the Gloucester Citizen, 9 April 1921:

'…better die of starvation in God's beautiful sunshine than go back to servile labour and semi-starvation caused by a wage that is not sufficient to keep a man …'

At that time, boys from the age of 14 worked in the mines, often as hod boys, crawling on their hands and knees in the dark and wet for 12 hours a day hauling a wooden tray of coal from the diggings to the trucks. The 1842 Mines Act banned women and children under the age of ten from the mines, and in 1900 this was extended to the age of thirteen. There is a beautiful sculpture commemorating these young boys set in a valley in the Forest of Dean.

WE BE STANDING HERE IN God's beautiful sunshine. Waiting for the hooter.

Middle o' summer, early, when the night's freshness baint yet dried out like sheets on a blowy wash day. The valley sides be heavy with green, glistering like the silk blouse our mam laundered for a wife from posh end o' the village. The way that blouse shimmied in the breezes is how the beech leaves shimmer with the sun on 'em.

All green up there. All brown and black down here. Buildings soot-smeared with coal dust, little slag heaps waiting to be carted away, black dirt underfoot. Won't be long afore we're black too—our clothes, our hands, our faces.

I look down at the hod by my boot. Empty o' coal these past months, it's a stranger. If'n you can say that 'bout a wood tray.

The birds chirrup and chirp, pleased with theirselves for being in the sunshine.

The chirruping and the whirring o' the pit head wheels be the only sounds. We doan say nothing. Nor look at each other. Shame and defeat silence even the loudest of hewers. Not that I'm allowed to speak. Not at fourteen.

We're waiting for the hooter.

Not heard the hooter for three months. The Doomsday-loud blast which harried us back down each and every single morning, down to the wet an' dark.

I was glad back then, early spring, when the hooter fell silent.

No more hodding!

No more lugging that burdensome tray behind me,

dreading the moment the straps was wrapped around my shoulders, the chain pulled between my legs. No more straining, sobbing for my mam to save me from agony, dragging that hod and its weight o' coal, belly, arms and knees shredded. Up to the light, brief-like, and down again to where the men are on their knees, or their sides, sweat-covered bare backs, hacking out black chunks to toss into my hod.

And do it all over again.

By then I'd learned to cry in the lonely blackness o' the tunnel, outta sight 'n hearing of the men, an' my sobs had quieted to mumbled sufferings. Scars and callouses hid my bloodied knees and elbows. But still I hated it, cursed the coal, the pits, the knowing there was no escape.

So the hooter's silence made me happy, although it shouldn't. Uncle Jim, my buttyman, he weren't happy. Nor the other men. Long faces an' me putting on a long face too. Pretending to be like the men.

Uncle Jim, being Mam's brother, took me on after Dad died falling off a cage in the shaft. Dad was supposed to teach me how it all worked, starting with the hod, then later the pick and drill. Forever on our knees or sides, no matter how old we got. If 'n we got old. Dad didn't. Old enough to leave Mam with ten of us though.

It weren't many days after Dad that we'd trudged home from the pits, grim-mouthed, through a Forest still winter-bare. Snow in patches. It must've been a Friday. I was carrying our portion o' coal which meant a warmer kitchen for a couple of days and a bath with hot, well, almost hot, water. Rumours, stories, buzzed in the frigid air like wasps 'round a bothered hive. I didn't fully understand, but I knowed summat was wrong by the angry murmurings.

Uncle Jim muttered 'bout all that great talk by Mr George promising a land fit for heroes, but nothing done, and now they doan want our coal any more. At least, not so much of it. Price of coal dropping like Dad off that cage and with the same deadly results. Bringing coal in from Germany. The men spat into the dirt. Germany? Didn't we just win the war to end all wars over them? Mebbe it was they who won.

It's not like the good times, during that great war, the men said. They needed our coal then, needed us. They stood taller, remembering as if it was a long ways past, not just three years.

I didn't stand tall, because I was a young 'un in the war, fetching water, seeing to the hens, feeding the pig, doing a bit o' school or shooting Germans with my butties in the beech woods behind Danby Lodge. It were good times for me too, but even better for the men. Dad smiling, bringing home cash each week, giving most of it to our mam, keeping his beer and baccy shillings for hisself. Back then, I knew it'd be a good thing when I got to hew the coal myself. I skipped over the hodding part, knowing that baint pretty. It wouldn't be fer long, I told myself. And then I'd be able to put food on the table every night, like Dad. In those days, we even had meat sometimes.

Some 'ave had meat these last months too. The ones his lordship's gamekeepers bain't catch ahold of. Plenty of rabbits for all in those warrens up there by the big house. But they doan like to share, do they?

We be waiting for the hooter, the minutes ticking by like the counting down to a hanging. No one's in a rush. The July sun's warm despite dawn weren't far back. I takes my cap off to get the heat on my head. Mebbe some of it'll stick, help out for a bit when I'm back in the cold. Mind you, you doan stay cold long hauling that hod up the tunnel.

Uncle Jim told Mam the rumours and the price dropping, and said t'was easy to see bad times coming. Mine owners' greediness and them in government not understanding. How could they? Uncle Jim tugged his beard. Never seen the outside of a mine more likely, least of all swing a pick in a foot and half of puddling blackness with a candle for light for twelve hours.

Bad times coming? As bad as me lugging that hod every day?

We watched the stockpiles by the pitheads grow tall like spoil heaps. No one to buy it for a decent price, Uncle Jim said. The men shook their heads and waited to be told it'd be part-time work from now. Like at Harrow Hill and Crown. Most of the men laid off there, and what they supposed to do? Nothing else going, now the tinplates works closed.

At night, I squeezed between my little brothers in the big iron bed and closed my eyes. Part time'd be good. Being laid off, even better.

No more hodding.

I were wise enough to kip my wishes to myself, seeing the worrit in Uncle Jim's eyes, and the way Mam's fingers fidgeted, twisting the ties of her apron or pulling at the strands of hair fallen out from her bun.

Mam's lips, already straight because of Dad, thinned further when she heard about the lay-offs. She didn't say nothing, but another sister got packed off to service too early.

Mam said to her: 'You old enough to earn your way now, Dotty, and likely we goin' need your wage even more'n need it now.'

Dotty cried all the way to the train, clutching her cardboard case with her spare stockings and petticoat to her chest like it was an anchor to home, and no doubt cried all the way to the big house in Cheltenham. She's twelve. She still drenches her pillow with tears every night she says in her letters, but she does it on a full tummy and in a bed all to herself. Lucky Dotty, is what I think. She'll get over being sick for home, like t'other girls do, coming back on an occasional Sunday to lord it over us with clean, new-like clothes and brushed hair.

Rose was already gone, after Dad fell off the cage. She went on her own all the way to London, being fifteen, a big girl, and better able to look after herself. She doan write much except the once, to tell us the lady is busy making sure women be allowed t'vote some time, so never at home, and the gentleman is kind, gives her little presents like ribbons and pretty buttons.

Mam breathed a bit fast when she read the letter. She didn't say nothing though, so I s'posed she was happy Rose had a kind master.

No kind masters for the men in the pits.

The stockpiles grew and then came the part-time work. Uncle Jim cut my wage more'n than the men's.

'Sorry,' he said to Mam. 'You've got summat

coming in, from the laundry and the girls, and I've got men with families who have to eat.'

Families like our neighbours, whose wives used t' share what they could with Mam, along with gossip. Paid-for bits o' mending and laundry, spare taters, a screw o' sugar or a candle nub. Nothing spare now, 'cepting our bodies.

I confess, glee warmed my gut when I realised there'd be less hodding, least for a while. But the glee were tainted. Uncle Jim knows Mam relies some on my small wage, so why weren't I deserving same consideration as men with families?

Mam didn't say nothing to Uncle Jim. She come inside and blew out the candle before scraping most coals out the fire. I'd piled 'em high as those stocks by pithead, she grumbled, and coal had to be rationed like sugar in the war. It were still winter and Jack Frost had his arms 'round the house good an' tight. Ice on the inside of the glass in the mornings, and the milk in the scullery froze. The hens looked right miserable and laid nothing.

The ransoms' pungent leaves along the stream were flourishing when Uncle Jim read the notice at the pithead. His pasty miner's face pastied whiter.

'All contracts done with end o' month,' he read aloud. Those who couldn't read or were too far back in t' crowd to see, waited to hear the rest. He read it to hisself, shook his head and turned to us all. 'No more government subsidies,' he said. 'Up to owners to decide what to pay from what the pits earn.' We listened harder. 'And owners say these be t' new contracts.' He looked us over from right to left. 'Half. Half what we being paid now, that's their new contract.'

The silence was a heartbeat and when it ended it was like the whooshing of the train coming outta Haie tunnel, all that pent up steam exploding like blasts in the mine.

'How we expected to keep a family on that?'

'My sister's man, he works the fields for near four times that! Sheer muscle is all he's got t' offer, no skills.'

I hardly listened, working it out. My wage'd be a fraction of the poverty-inducing money hewers and buttymen would get. I'd be on my belly all day for nigh on nothing. How'd that help Mam?

Misery sunk deep into my scratched belly. I wanted to sob like in the beginning, this time for knowing the uselessness of it all.

Our miners tain't easily cowed, mind. End of month come, and the men held out. Be reduced to starvation? No. A tiny flicker of hope, like a match struck underground, sparked in me. Perhaps it wouldn't be all useless after all.

But they owners, they locked us out. No going t'mines at all.

Big part of me was glad, couldn't help it. My misery took itself on holiday. No more crying to ease t' agony in knees and elbows, and that chain chafing. Not forever, but free for now.

It weren't all gladness though. I were smart enough to know no more hodding meant no more cash. Not even the part wage from Uncle Jim.

It weren't so bad to start and I let my gladness grow. Were winter veg in the store, the pig and chickens. We didn't go too hungry. Then Mam's laundry work dried up because who could pay for laundry? And Rose come home, turning up sudden with her case and no reference, crying endlessly, not saying why.

Uncle Jim helped. He's got his own to look out for, eight o' them. That's not 'cluding the four died when they was small. Sad. We had two died. I was too little to understand, just grateful the thin wailing stopped and there were an inch more space to wriggle in the bed.

The craftsmen backed the men. Wouldn't kip the pumps going, and in our Forest pumps are king, perhaps more'n coal. No pumping, no coal. Uncle Jim said perhaps the owners'd give in then.

'Flooding!' the Mercury headlined. 'Whole coalfield in danger!'

Gallons o' water streamed through the tunnels, overflowing the carts, dousing the electrics where there were any.

I worrited then.

'The ponies!'

Mam shook her head and I worrited more, but, 'They got 'em out, son, doan thee worrit about ponies, they's having a holiday in Crumpmeadow.'

I breathed. Me and the ponies understand each other, hauling great loads of coal uphill in the wet dark all day. And we both having holidays.

His lordship got his hands dirty then, he and other rich men manning pumps. Wonder they knew how. Mam showed me photos in the Mercury. She didn't say nothing. Didn't have to. It's their mines. We woulda done same if our house was flooding.

We're waiting for the hooter. The sun burns hot as red ash on my head an' I clamp my cap back on. I shuffle my boots, coal dust rising to blunt their shine, make 'em more familiar. Seems we been waiting for that hooter a long time. I glance at Uncle Jim, next to me. He's studying the dirt, hands in his coat pockets. He tosses me a quick sideways look and his eyes are anxious.

Are they going t' let us back in?

They wasn't going to, earlier.

Uncle Jim come by with a slice off a flitch of bacon. He told Mam there be rumours they closing the mines for good.

Mam stared and Uncle Jim shrugged. 'If they t'aint profitable, why kip 'em open?'

Mam didn't say nothing, just lifted the youngest from her jutting hip to the floor, sent it on its toddling way to play with a brother or sister in the yard.

'They doan care how a man can feed his family.' Uncle Jim scowled, rubbed his beard with fingers still coal-blackened. 'They be capitalists, care only for money.'

My stupid heart jumped. The glee part let itself fully loose. If they closed the mines, hodding'd be gone, forever. Mam and Uncle Jim were afraid, and I should be too, but summat in me rejoiced.

I'd go away, join the army like Dad wanted to in the war, only they needed him in the mines. That made me a little glad too, Dad not being here to see how they doan need him no more.

That night Mam's lips were pinched tight. After

feeding us thin bread with a scrape o' blackberry jam, she stared into the sullen fire with her hands in her lap. It were so unlikely, her not mending or peeling or scrubbing or washing, that I worrited she was sickening. The middle 'uns got the little 'uns into the bed without taking 'em to the dunny or washing their jam-smeared cheeks. Mam sat idle, which made me worrit more. She must be hurting somewhere deep inside to not look to the little 'uns.

A prick of guilt poked my conscience when I thought 'bout it. If 'n there was no mines, there'd be no work, and no work meant not enough cash all 'round so men could feed their families and have a little spare so widows like Mam had a hope of making do. My glee soured in my mouth, like eating scrump apples.

Mam were up early next morning, heating water to scrub pee-stained kids and sheets, so she weren't sickening. But I worrited still.

It weren't the only time they owners said they'd close whole coalfield. All right for them, with their big houses and carriages and shiny top hats. No thought for us.

I hoped they might learn, the day the families showed how they stuck with the men.

Mam didn't say nothing, only patched and washed the little 'uns breeches, shirts and frocks, polished their shoes and joined the women and kids, more than anyone could count. We marched to Speech House, overflowing the big field in drabby imitation of the bluebells filling the beech woods like a summer sky laid on the ground. We listened real careful to important men haranguing the owners and government. They weren't there o' course t' hear, but their ears must've burned red.

Didn't do no good.

None of us was fat to start with and soon the crying of the little 'uns going to bed hungry was wearing my nerves. I was hungry too. Hungry enough to think of hodding as a good thing, if it'd stop the wailing.

The County laid on school dinners which helped because by then the pig was gone, the hens too, except a couple for an occasional precious egg. Good thing some of the posh people was on our side, setting up soup kitchens. Having to beg for our dinner, which is how Mam saw it, was hard. Never had to do that afore.

'It's not begging, our mam,' I said. 'Pretend it's like the chapel picnic, remember the once we went?' I wanted her to feel better about it, not lose her pride. Seemed the only thing I could do.

Mam huffed and didn't say nothing, but I knew she was thinking 'bout her embarrassment at that picnic with our shabby trousers and frocks, even with them cleaned to within a shred of their threadbare lives. Never went again. Not chapel goers, not without a rag to our backs good enough t' wear. The chapel folk helped anyway and Mam was grateful though she not said nothing except to wag a finger at the little 'uns and warn 'em to be sure and say thank 'ee when they got their bread and soup.

Sun's so heated now I want to shed my coat while we wait for the hooter. Can't put it on the filthy ground though. Mam brushed it last night, and I was made to polish my boots.

Mam didn't say nothing. She didn't have to. Clear as a shout was what she was thinking: If you have to go back, you do it with pride.

Our Mam's uncertain 'bout us going back. It's the big union's orders, despite the men pointing out how we be worse off than afore.

'It's go back, or no more pits at all,' they told us.

Not just the owners this time. Our own big union bosses saying it too. The rest of the country caved in, not strong like us.

'Less to lose,' Uncle Jim muttered. 'More profits to pay decent wages.'

The women would've held out. Even with their kids going hungry, because we all going to go hungry anyway.

But – I take a deep breath standing there in the sunshine – not as hungry as we been these last months.

It's unjust. Those greedy owners got us in the end. But not because of us men here. We can hold our heads up, brag they owners' threats didn't cow us. That's what I want to say, to wipe away the black looks of shame, of defeat. If anyone'd listen to a hod boy.

The hooter blares, blasting the chirruping birds into a squawking like Yorkley brass tuning up.

I glance at Uncle Jim whose lips twitch in the tiniest o' smiles. I grin, quick, and lift my chin, hitch my trousers and my shoulders and take up my hod.

We tramp alongside t' other men with God's beautiful sunshine warming us.

It's back to hodding. It baint going t'hurt any less. The callouses'll be back afore long. But there'll be cash for more'n hard bread and scrape of jam for

Mam and the kids.

I be providing for my family, like t'other men. Dad'd be proud.

Sabrina rising

Winner, Secret Attic monthly competition August 2020, and selected for Stroud Short Stories May 2021. Previously published in Dragon Gift, Secret Attic Booklet 4# *and* Stroud Short Stories Anthology Vol 3

The Great Flood of 30 January 1607 devastated both sides of the Bristol Channel and the Severn Estuary with flooding as far as Gloucester. An estimated 500-1000 people and thousands of livestock perished.

AGNES HAS A HEADACHE. THE thick air presses her temples, her heavy-lidded eyes squint despite the lack of sun. She glances up, for the hundredth time that morning. Black clouds broil above the fields, frothing like a mad dog's spit, resisting the wet wind tossing them across a purple sky to merge with the distant mountains. The wind is false, mild, non-wintry.

Agnes crosses herself and returns to raking out the pig's sty. The Devil has been let loose from Hell this morning. Her thoughts go to Evan, fishing on the river. He's a farmer, not a fisherman, but the rare higher tide today has tempted him. Lamprey for our supper tonight, he told her with his big grin when he left in the darkness. The river will run fast. Agnes shivers. She never trusts the river. It might be called Severn these days but Agnes has heard the heathen Romans called the river Sabrina, worshipped her as a goddess and the Good Lord knows she's every bit as temperamental as any goddess. Agnes crosses herself again.

She finishes her raking, slow and clumsy with her big belly, bloated with child. She throws fresh straw into the sty, refills the water trough. The pig crouches in a corner, tiny eyes watching her. It seems wary, as if Agnes is a stranger come to do it harm. Not yet, piggy, not yet.

Agnes presses one hand to her throbbing head, another to her belly, and returns the pig's stare before waddling across the yard to the farmhouse. The hens cluck around her legs, fluffing their feathers. Agnes impatiently pushes the most persistent aside with her boot. They follow her inside, cackling as if their necks are about to be wrung. Agnes scowls. Their necks might well be wrung, if they keep this up.

'Lewis,' she says to her six-year-old, and the oldest, 'did you search all over for eggs? These idiot birds will have laid them in any hole or under any bush today.'

'Yes, Ma.' Lewis pokes the fire with a stick and reaches for the last of the wood piled by the hearth.

Agnes sighs, pulls her shawl tighter and peers into the cradle where baby Rhys sleeps. She strokes his fat pink cheek. A beautiful baby, quiet. An angel.

'Where is Gwillim?' Agnes says. 'Is he fetching wood?'

Lewis shakes his head. 'He wanted to go fishing with Da.'

A cold finger slides down the nape of Agnes' neck. Gwillim is four, and fearless. 'He's gone to the river?'

Lewis shrugs.

'Then you must fetch the wood while I find him. A storm is coming, a violent storm. He'll be blown away if he's caught out in it.'

She goes into the yard and looks up, again, at the sky. The wind pulls at her uncapped hair to send it swirling about her head like the swirling of lampreys in the river.

'Stupid, stupid Evan,' she mutters. 'Stupid, stupid Gwillim'.

Her chest tightens and she runs into the wind, through the gate in the stone wall which protects her vegetables from the sheep, and along the path to the river.

She stops. Water races towards her. It covers the path and spreads to the left and the right, churning in a froth of brown and dirty white like storm waves on the seashore.

But it's not the blue sea. Agnes recognises the colours of the river, which, it seems, reached its high tide and wasn't content to stop. Instead it has swelled like Agnes' stomach until it's burst the non-too-sturdy defences meant to keep it to its own banks.

Evan? Gwillim? Agnes can't breathe.

She steps forward, into the water, and is knocked to her backside. It rises, rises, and Agnes is pushed and dragged, straining to stand but her belly and her sodden skirts drag her, the river tumbling her like a stone. A sheep floats past, legs scrabbling, terror-wide eyes rolling. It bleats. There's more bleating, the heartrending cries joining together to lift above the silence of the rising waters, to cut through the braying of the wind.

Agnes heaves against the water, pushes her arms forward and finds the stone wall. She presses her shaking body against it and cries as loudly as the drowning sheep when the water churns through the gate, swift as a spring stream, and into the house.

'Lewis!'

The wind whips her thin voice away but Lewis is there, by the door, his knees submerged.

'The table!' Agnes yells, terror finally giving her strength to shout. 'Climb on the table!'

Lewis nods, bright boy, while Agnes prays to God that the table, weighed down with Lewis and the iron pot Agnes had been about to fill with dinner, won't float.

Rhys! The cradle is on the floor by the fire. It will float, and Lewis will grab it, hold it against the water, keep his baby brother safe. Agnes' body shakes harder, and not from cold alone.

Her hands and feet grow numb, terror pounds her heart against her ribs, but still she clings to the wall. The water rises up her legs, to her waist, spilling over the stones to level itself either side of her fragile sanctuary. She is half-blinded by her hair, can hear nothing except wind and water and screaming sheep, but she turns her head, praying for a sight of Evan striding through the swirling muck, Gwillim on his shoulders.

What she sees instead is the cradle, and she is sick at the knowledge that the water inside the house has reached the window. Her baby son sails out of view and Agnes pushes herself along the wall, stone by stone. Her feet barely touch the ground, the water eddies around her like a whirlpool sucking her into its depths.

If Evan was here, he could swim to the cradle. But Evan is on the river, in the river. With Gwillim. And Agnes can't swim.

She clutches the stones and joins her screams to the cacophony of the sheep.

...

It's near dark when the wind drops to tired squalls and the water recedes enough to let a trembling Agnes squelch to the mud-filled house. Lewis is there, crouched on the table with four fright-struck hens gathered tight against his legs. Agnes takes the boy, hens and all, in her shivering arms.

'I couldn't get to him, Ma.' Lewis sobs into her chest.

'I know, I know.' Neither could Agnes. She knows Lewis' pain.

'Da?' Lewis says. 'Gwillim?'

Agnes shakes her head. 'They will come if they come,' she says and gulps back sobs for Lewis' sake. 'But now I have to see about the pig and the cow.' She sets the boy and the hens on the floor, takes Lewis' hand. It's unspoken that she won't leave him alone, not this time.

The cow is gone, but the pig is on the roof of its sty, lifted by the water, kept alive by the higher walls on three sides. It stares at Agnes with accusing tiny eyes. It had been right to be wary.

'We have the pig still,' Agnes says to Lewis.

'And the hens I saved.' He takes her hand and offers a trembling, fleeting, smile.

Agnes cups her free hand beneath her belly. She feels life there too.

The making of a wise woman

Longlisted in the Historical Writers Association 2020 short story competition. Subsequently became Cheryl's award-winning novel River Witch.

The Romans knew the River Severn as Sabrina and revered her as a goddess. Fishing was a major industry until quite recently. The busy port of Shiphaven is a thinly disguised Newnham-on-Severn.

THE MAN IS TALKING TO the river. He's tall and hatless with straight black hair to his shoulders. His long coat is shiny at the elbows and his yellow brocade waistcoat is frayed around the buttonholes.

Hester decides he must be, or once was, a gentleman because she sees gentlemen in the village and they wear long coats and waistcoats. She's noticed the frayed buttonholes even though she's only six years old because her mother mends buttonholes for money. The farm is not enough, despite the long hours her strong father works. Not with eight of them to clothe and feed.

But what makes Hester eye the man with piqued curiosity is that he's talking to the river. Talking to the river is Hester's job.

Or rather, the river talks to her. When the river is low it whispers, shushing its way over the sandbanks like the silks her mother sews shush over Hester's hands. Then, as the tide comes in, the waters swoosh and swirl like storm clouds, but steadier, swifter, louder, and the swans and gulls hitch fast rides alongside the trows.

All the time, the river talks to Hester. The river tells her she is a good girl, which is what Father says when Hester finds the eggs the hens hide or wakes in the night to feed the motherless lamb by the kitchen fire. The river tells her that it and Hester are one, the same, spilling over the mudbanks and lapping the stony cliffs together – always.

The man takes two long steps towards Hester. His black hair glistens like raven feathers in the bright sun. Gold flecks glint in his dark eyes.

'Hello, Mistress Hester.' He bows formally, even though he doesn't have a hat to doff.

Hester stares. She would put her thumb in her mouth only Mother has beaten the habit out of her and Hester daren't renew it.

The man keeps smiling. 'You come to the river often, don't you?'

Hester nods.

'I've seen you here, talking to Sabrina.'

Who, where, is this Sabrina? Hester turns her head so quickly her untidy curls slap her cheek.

The man laughs. 'Sabrina is the name of the river,' he says, gesturing towards the placid wide stream flowing at this moment down to the sea.

(Hester imagines the sea as numerous rivers mingling side by side, haphazardly running off to the edge of the world in the same way Mother's ribbons fall tangled over the edge of her sewing basket.)

Hester shakes her head. 'That's not the name of the river,' she says. 'It's got another name …' She frowns.

'You mean the name the ordinary folk call it?'

'Yes.'

'You and I are not ordinary folk, Hester. We are wise. And we call the river by her goddess name, Sabrina.'

'God?'

'No, goddess.' The man comes closer to Hester. 'Shall we go?' He offers his hand for Hester to take, if she wishes.

Hester looks at the hand, which doesn't go away, so she takes it and the man leads her alongside the hedgerows and tells her the names of the flowers growing at the edge of the fields and sprouting from the hedges themselves.

'Here is yarrow.' His long fingers caress the froth of lilac flowers which remind Hester of the lacy trims Mother sews on hems. 'Cures colds,' he says. 'And toothache.'

He holds a white flower to Hester's nose. She sniffs and her eyes crinkle. 'I know this one,' she says. 'Meadowsweet. Mother says I'll carry meadowsweet when I marry.'

'Marry?' The man raises a dark eyebrow. 'Does she, now?'

He collects feverfew and says, 'I'll dry these and

when I see you next I'll make you a present of them. They'll make you strong.'

Hester wants to be strong, like Father.

...

The autumn sun is young enough to retain summer's warmth and Hester dawdles past thinning hedgerows while she ponders the latest of the wise man's lessons. Marking a milestone in her years of learning, Hester was trusted with brewing a potion of belladonna, the dried berries blended with holy water from the sacred well which the wise man carries down from the forested hills. She recalls the hot day he and she harvested the shiny black fruit, stored with care and Hester's hands bathed afterwards with honey-scented tallow soap. Belladonna, he told Hester with a lift of his dark eyebrow, aids in forgetting past loves.

Hester is on her way to the field with Father's dinner. She hasn't eaten since milking and her stomach roils at the smell of the warm bread in her basket. Her fingers find their own way under the cloth to tear at the grainy loaf. She pops the stolen crumbs into her mouth and swallows without chewing, as if her lack of savouring the morsel will negate the sin of the theft. Another sin to add to the long list with which her brothers taunt her.

'Lazy Hester,' they say when they find her by the river talking with Sabrina. 'Idling your time away. Our father spoils you, girl. He should be reminding you that there are cows to be milked and butter to be churned. Back to your chores.'

'Fey,' they snigger when Hester sets down her sewing needle to follow the fire's sparks spitting their escape up the black chimney. But Father's eyes smile at Hester from over his clay pipe.

'Wilful,' the brothers claim when she refuses to respond to their hounding about where she goes when her tasks are (mostly) done. Her brothers would, but cannot, follow her. The wise man has seen to that. 'Lovers' tryst?' they used to tease but the teasing has turned to scowls since Hester grew to young womanhood, still with untidy curls.

Hester cannot see Father in the field. She sees the plough, the harnessed horses standing quietly, flicking their tails. She frowns, and runs.

Father lies spread on the ground behind the plough. His arms are flung wide and his eyes stare into the sun. She stands over him, banging the basket against her skirts, taking great gasping sobs.

Her strong father! No!

'Hello, Hester.'

The man is there, summoned by Hester's need. She drops the basket and blinks at him.

'Is he dead?' she says between sobs.

The man squats down, presses his fingers to Father's neck, lays his too-long dark hair on Father's unmoving chest.

'I'm sorry, Hester.'

'Raise him!' Hester says. 'You're a wise man … return him to me!'

He shakes his head.

Hester's mind gallops. 'Bergamot? Rue and rosemary?' she pleads. She beats her fists on his chest. 'Tell me! There must be something! There must!'

The man takes Hester's hands in his own and presses their bunched fists to his yellow waistcoat, much faded now but with the buttonholes neatly mended by Hester herself. She leans her head against him and cries her pain.

'No, Hester,' the wise man murmurs into Hester's hair. 'You know this. You know there is no tincture, no potion to raise the dead. You must be strong, Hester. Remember, you are not ordinary folk.'

Hester leans away and reaches inside her gown to crush the muslin bag of dried feverfew she always wears. It doesn't make her strong, doesn't ease her pain.

'Go home, let them know.' The wise man glances up at circling ravens. 'I will watch until you return. And afterwards, Sabrina will comfort you.'

...

The farmhouse fills with women laying out Father's body while comforting Mother. Hester's brothers rebuke themselves with pursed mouths and angry eyes. One of them should have been ploughing the field, not Father.

'No,' Mother says. She embraces each in turn. 'Father loved his alone time with the soil and the sky and the horses. God took him at his best.'

Hester is jealous that God may choose when is the best.

The funeral service is made longer by the icy chill instilled deep in the ancient church's flagged floors and stone walls. Hester clasps her gloved hands together more in an effort to warm them than in piety. Mother sits beside her. A new veil made of dressmaking leftovers disguises an old hat and her Sunday best black gown has been sponged into cleanliness.

In the cemetery, Hester stares down the slope to the river. Sabrina flows fast to the sea, her waters thick with sails and plumes of steam trailing like kite tails. A cattle boat is being hauled across by the ferry and the cows low their panic into the air. The goddess does nothing to soothe them. Instead, she reaches out to Hester, the damp wind carrying her message: 'Be strong, Hester, be strong.' Hester presses her hand against her chest where the feverfew lies.

Opposite Hester, her brothers glare at the coffin as it's lowered into the earth and Mother throws the first clods onto the shiny wood.

Tomorrow Hester, Mother and the brothers will leave their tenant farm. They will live in the village, in a house where Mother and Hester will sew dresses for the shopkeepers' and merchants' wives. Hester has no wish to sew dresses. She wishes to sell herbs and potions but Mother and her brothers shrink from the idea.

'Witch!' the brothers accuse her.

The older brothers introduce the younger ones to their new trades of fishing and brickmaking and it's from one of these trades that Hester receives the attentions of her first beau. The visitor is dressed neatly in dark trousers, a clean collar on his shirt and a brushed coat. His shoes shine like belladonna berries. He twists his hat in his fishhook-scarred hands and mumbles his thanks to Mother for the tea.

Hester and the fisherman walk the river path and Sabrina whispers in Hester's ear: 'Be strong, Hester. You are not ordinary folk. You are not for the likes of him.'

The fisherman lunges at Hester, wraps his arms about her and kisses her, hard, on her surprised open mouth. He has salmon breath. Hester pushes him away with a mocking laugh.

'Why?' she says.

'Why not?' the fisherman says. 'We'll wed and I'll kiss you whenever I wish.'

'Will you?' Hester laughs again. She lifts her skirts and runs through the mud, up the lane and into the street where the merchants' and shopkeepers' windows light her way.

Behind her, the fisherman laughs too.

'Well?' Mother sits in the candle's circle of light. She sets aside the collar she is edging with green ribbon and rubs her eyes.

'Well what?'

'When will you marry?'

'Marry?' Hester throws out a hand. 'Him?' Her stomach twists.

'Yes, him.' Mother sighs. 'Your brothers pay their way. But you, Hester, pay nothing and are never here to help with the sewing or the chores. The Lord alone knows where you go.'

Hester moves to the fire although she doubts its poor flames will warm her sudden chill.

'Since we've come into the village,' Mother says, 'there's gossip about you.'

'Gossip?' Sabrina whispers in Hester's ear: 'Be strong.'

'Yes.' Mother's voice is weary. 'They ask me if you're sickly, if you suffer from visions, as they see you walking by the river talking to yourself.'

'And you tell them...?'

'I tell them you grieve for your father, I tell them you are a spiritual young woman. I tell them a sturdy husband and lusty babies will settle you, the sooner the better.' Mother rises from the chair and takes up the candle. 'You will marry the fisherman, Hester.'

Hester's world darkens.

...

From her bedroom window Hester watches the flames of the Samhain fire cast the louring clouds in pink. A heavy wind offers the noises and smells of the celebration to her like an unwanted gift: the ordinary folk cheering and laughing, the fiddles screeching, the smell of scorched wood with undertones of beer and cider. Her mother and brothers are there. Soon the lumpen fisherman will knock on the door, confident, brash, demanding Hester take his oar-like arm and dance smiling around the fire like any maiden about to be married with her posy of meadowsweet.

Hester's breath catches in her gorge. 'Be strong,' she whispers.

She runs through the cobbled lanes down to the river. She carries a lantern which swings like a call for help as she takes the sliver of path out of the village, through the tall reeds to the emptiness beyond. Hatless, her curls tug at their roots as if demanding the freedom of gulls. Hester stops, the lantern at her feet, breathing in the river and staring across the waters. She waits for Sabrina's murmurs.

Sabrina is as low, grey and swift as the sky. Trows nestling against the far bank until the tide's turning are defined by their lights while the ferry lights quiver on the undulating surface like captive stars.

'Hello, Hester.'

The wise man is there, summoned by Hester's need. They stand side by side, close. He smells of apples and fire.

'What does Sabrina say tonight?' he says.

Hester listens. The voice of the river murmurs to her, straining through the wind, trying to be heard.

'She is sorry for my unhappiness,' Hester says, although she is unsure of this. Sabrina has never been a consoling goddess. 'She says I am to be strong, as she was when the soldiers threw her into the waters and the nymphs blessed her with divinity.'

The wise man has taught Hester more than herbs and potions.

'Does this mean I should follow her? Throw myself into the river?'

The wise man humphs. 'That is one path, Hester. But you are stronger than that.' He offers his arm for Hester to take, if she wishes. She lays her hand on it. 'Come now,' he says. 'There is another learning waiting for you. If you choose to embrace it, you will take a different path. A harder path.' He covers Hester's hand with his own, un-gloved one.

Hester lets him lead her away. Her heart thumps.

...

The sun wakens her, creeping across her pillow like a weakened kitten. Hester is in her own bed. She half-opens her eyes, closes them again and pulls her knees up to her stomach, her arms hugging her breasts. Her memories are sweetly fuddled.

'Will you drink?' The wise man had offered Hester a clay cup which steamed in the cool air of the cottage. Hester took the cup and breathed the grassiness of Lady's Mantle, the citrus tang of lemon balm. A glass jar of poppy seeds sat by the mortar among dried yellow flowers and curling leaves.

A potion of love and lust.

And, Hester knew, more, much more. Other magic crouched in the warm liquid – magic to carry her into the shadowlands, to commune with spirits, to soar with them like the gulls fly with the winds. She had let out a shuddering breath and drunk from the cup, one long swallow, staring into gold-flecked eyes which clawed deep into her being, snatching at her soul.

The leaping, sparking fire had mocked the tawdry village flames and heated the sweat-slicked arms and legs tangled on the hearth mat. Too-long dark hair feathered like ravens' wings brushed Hester's burning face and her tongue sought the sulphurous odour which settled on her lips. She grasped the power, savouring the dizzy joy.

Afterwards there was the night sky, the white moon chasing the tempestuous clouds. Hester rode above the river, laughing, her cheek hot against the wise man's back. The wind whirled her hair into the silvered darkness, the spirits pressed against her and an exultant Sabrina called, 'You are strong, Hester.'

Now Hester pushes back the blanket and peers down at her languorous body. It appears to be the same body as yesterday, although clothed in chemise and drawers rather than a nightgown. Her dress and cloak are folded on the chair under the open window. Hester sits up and swings her legs over the side of the bed. She winces.

When she throws the blanket fully back, she sees the spot of blood which stains her sheet.

Hester stares at the spot and licks at the taste of sulphur on her lips. Her pulse quickens. Her path is chosen.

...

Mother refuses to allow Hester out of the house. The villagers bring their gowns to reshape to new fashions and breeches and skirts to let out for growing children. They cast sidelong glances at Hester and ask Mother about the girl's health in loud whispers. Mother tells them Hester and the fisherman will marry in the spring and a sturdy husband and lusty babies will soon set Hester to rights. Hester cannot wait, Mother says.

Hester bends closer over her needle, as if in modesty.

The snow is deep. The wind howls across the river and shakes the thin glass in the windows in its frustration at not being allowed in. Hester wakes in darkness and works beyond the setting of the winter sun, finishing each day rubbing eyes made sore by the flickering tallow of the cheap candles.

Mother is grateful.

'You're a good daughter after all, Hester,' she says and Hester smiles and threads her needle in the smoky light.

Her body has kept its languorous contentment and she sews absently, her mind cavorting with secret, gleeful half-visions. She stretches like a cat before the fire and agrees with Mother that she cannot wait for spring.

Her brothers watch her with narrowed eyes, as if she is an imposter and where is their fey sister? They don't ask, believing the idea of marriage has settled her wildness.

But as winter moves with its usual sluggish pace towards spring, Hester feels more changes in her body. At night she touches her swollen breasts and counts back ... During the day, Mother tilts her head and says, 'Love is making you bloom, Hester. You will be a beautiful bride with your posy of meadowsweet.'

Hester shrinks into her chair. She fingers the bag of feverfew and stares at the fire, reliving gold-flecked eyes and the night wind in her hair to smother images of fish-hook scarred hands and salmon breath. She harvests her strength for all the courage she can reap.

While the household sleeps, Hester wraps herself in her cloak and quietly unlatches the door. The night is lit with frozen stars lorded over by a full moon. Hester runs past the inns where the sailors' and fishermen's bawdy songs stumble drunkenly into the road, praying the lustful singers won't decide now is the time to seek their trows and huts.

She runs past Father's grave and across fields where sheep glimmer white in the darkness, her boots slipping in the mud. A hunting owl calls encouragement, steadying her. Hester stands on the cliffs above the river with her cloak wrapped about her, reaches into her gown for the muslin-wrapped feverfew, and waits.

When he doesn't come, Hester's courage frays like cut rope. He's telling her she must marry the fisherman, have babies, make Mother happy. Assure the villagers Hester is ordinary folk, like them.

The wind from the river lifts Sabrina's voice: 'You are not ordinary folk, Hester. You chose your path on Samhain. You are strong.'

'I am strong,' Hester whispers.

...

His cottage above the river shows no light. Hester tries the latch and the door opens wide, welcoming her. No flames leap, but the moon sends a stream of silver through the window to light up the table and the shelves, the stripped bed and the two chairs by the swept fireplace.

The shelves which held the results of Hester's lessons are empty. The table where she spent countless tranquil hours is not bare, however. A glass jar of dried leaves labelled Raspberry Leaf stands there. Here is a choice: raspberry leaf can solve Hester's problem right now, or it can help later to ease her birthing pangs. She presses both hands against her stomach.

Next to the jar stands the mortar and pestle and a newly stitched muslin bag which Hester knows will contain freshly dried feverfew. And hard by the feverfew is the stone bottle of belladonna potion.

'To forget past loves,' Hester murmurs. She lifts it. Only a little remains.

There is one other item in the cottage – a besom broom leans into the corner by the fireplace.

Hester runs a hand through her curls and smiles.

There is only the night sky, the white moon sailing the tempestuous clouds as smoothly as the wherry gliding on its great cables across the river below. Hester rides with the wind whirling her hair into the silvered darkness, laughing, feeling the muslin bag warm against her skin.

Sabrina reaches up, whispering: 'You are strong, Hester.'

In the moonlit cottage, the jar of raspberry leaf sits unopened on the table. The stone bottle? Its shards lie scattered on the wet flags of the floor.

St Ceyna whispers

A variation on a scene from River Witch. *The real well in the Forest of Dean, St Anthony's, is reputed to have healing powers, and even now people bottle its waters.*

THE RHYTHM OF THE MARE lulls Catherine into a dream-like state. The September sun is too young to soften summer's heat, yet the air beneath the trees breathes coolness like a living creature. It's as if ancient eyes measure her progress through the forest, gracious ghosts encouraging her with whispers and soft flutterings of hands on her back. Perhaps the spirit of St Ceyna herself approves this forbidden excursion to her well.

Molly flicks her mane and snickers softly. Catherine keeps on, the guilty beating of her heart which has accompanied her out of the house, up the track and into the forest, quieting the closer she comes to the waters she longs for.

...

Mrs Bryce had handed Catherine a tall glass of tepid elderflower cordial.

'What you need, Miss Catherine,' she said, 'is cordial made with water from the well.'

'Which well?'

'The sacred well. St Ceyna's.' Mrs Bryce folded her arms under her bosom. 'Powerful stuff. When my ma was ill with milk fever with the youngest, 'twas the saint's water cured her. Granny Williams used it in her fenugreek poultice.'

'Perhaps it was the fenugreek which righted your mother? Did the water matter?'

Mrs Bryce arched her brows. 'It did, Miss Catherine, it did. And now I must attend to dinner before your father is home asking why he must wait for his meal.'

Catherine had set the cordial on a side table which also held a lawn handkerchief she was supposedly embroidering. With her skull feeling as if it had been stuffed with sheep's wool, sewing was impossible in the hot airlessness of noon. She lifted her legs onto the sofa, lay against a cushion and closed her eyes. Her mind wandered to St Ceyna's deep, dark waters. Her body relaxed, her breathing deepened as she sank into the well's imagined, languorous coolness.

Papa had first taken her there when she was eight years old. It was autumn. Catherine's pony breathed frosted drops into the air while its hooves crunched the red and gold leaves carpeting the ground as richly as any Turkish rug at home.

'Who was St Ceyna?' Catherine had asked.

Papa stroked his beard. 'A Welsh princess, from long, long ago. Very beautiful, yet she never married and lived as a hermitess most of her life.' He gave her a sideways glance, smiling. 'Some say she talked with the spirits of the forest and the streams.'

Catherine had stared into the clear, icy pool, conjuring a long-haired beauty bathing under a silver moon.

They had been three times since, in the days before Catherine's wearying illness kept her tethered to the house as if she were a cow in a byre. On this perspiring day the leaves sheltering the well would be dark with the mature green of late summer. A penultimate taste of life before the final glittering display, a last burst of joy, heralded their death in the frozen nights.

She roused herself sufficiently to sip the cordial. How might it feel to glitter with joy before death? If she is dying – as she thinks she might be – she badly wants to glitter first, instead of this lethargic fading away she can do nothing to dispel.

...

'Will you take me to St Ceyna's?' Catherine sat stiffly upright on the sofa. It took effort to hold herself straight for so long, but Papa would deny her immediately unless she showed how robust, how well, she felt.

'Why do you wish to go there?' Papa put aside his newspaper and frowned from his chair by the side of the empty fireplace.

Catherine filled her voice with desperate pleading. 'Because, Papa, I am tired of staying in the house. I need to see somewhere different before winter locks us in forever.' She clasped her hands beneath her chin. 'Please?'

'Impossible! The carriage can't get us there, the track is too narrow and overhung. It can't be done.'

He waved his pipe. 'You are unwell, Catherine. Doctor Newton says you must rest. Gallivanting off into the forest is not resting.'

Catherine pulled in her lips. 'If I rest any longer I shall die of boredom long before I die of whatever it is that ails me.'

'Daughter!'

Catherine sighed. 'I can ride Molly. I do remember how to ride. It's not far.'

'You will make do with the carriage and a short promenade along the river.' Papa lifted the newspaper and turned a page. 'Not the well.'

Catherine's stomach turned over. All those people jostling their not-always-clean bodies close to her, greeting each other with loud cheeriness and banal chat.

'Thank you.' She wriggled into the sofa to ease her aching shoulders. 'But I will stay here and dream of St Ceyna instead.'

And dream she did while her longing to visit the well grew into an obsession through the last days of August. In her dreams she floated on the waters, knowing the caress of icy wetness soothing her arms and legs, sliding silken across her naked body. Her head thrown back, her light blonde hair trailed its lengths on the still surface as St Ceyna's dark hair did all those centuries ago. She would wake in a twist of damp nightgown and sheets, flushing at the memory of her own dreamed nakedness.

Catherine's desire, her desperation, could not wait on permission.

...

A path weaves in leisurely loops between blunt-edged quarried stones, clumps of fern and stands of bracken up to a ridge. Here, the narrow valley which was home to St Ceyna falls away to a thin, straight stream which feeds the sacred well. The beech and oak are as Catherine remembers: thick with age, entwined branches shelter the rough stone rectangle of the well in imitation of twisted trusses sustaining a church roof above a nave.

She hesitates at the trees' edge. Someone else is here. A girl with a tumble of dark curls falling over her cheeks, kneels above the water to dip a pitcher. Mottled sunlight shimmers on her arched body as if she is attended by dancing water sprites.

Catherine watches, delighted. Has she been granted a vision of St Ceyna?

The girl sets the pitcher on the ground and turns to see who has intruded her aloneness.

No vision after all. Here is a sturdy farmer's daughter, or perhaps she belongs to a shopkeeper. She is dressed well, but plainly, in a blue short-sleeved calico frock with a white collar. Her feet are bare. A pair of black boots stuffed with white stockings are lined up neatly not far away.

'Hello,' the girl says. 'Have you come to collect water?'

'No.'

'To bathe?'

The girl jumps to her feet and comes closer. The dappled sunlight follows her and Catherine peers closely, unsurprised if fairies really did play about her head and shoulders.

When the girl strokes Molly's nose, the mare submits with more than her usual grace. She relaxes under the caresses, ears forward. A farmer's daughter then?

'No, not to bathe.' Catherine grows hot, momentarily reliving her dreams. 'At least, only to bathe my face and hands and maybe dip my feet, to cool them, to cool myself.'

'I did that, before I filled the pitcher.' The girl brushes aside a wet strand of curls. 'The water's so cold it makes your skin tingle.' She breathes softly into Molly's nostrils. 'You're beautiful, aren't you?'

Molly whickers her agreement.

Catherine laughs. 'You have an excellent way with horses. I'd swear she understood you.'

The girl glances up, a smile tugging at her lips and a keen emotion, perhaps pride, flows across her cornflower blue eyes.

'Can you dismount by yourself?' she says.

Catherine hesitates. 'I can, but'–here is the flaw in her plan–'I'm not sure I'll be able to re-mount. It's a long way to walk home.'

'I'll help you.' The girl squares her shoulders. 'I'm strong.' She points to a wide, uneven stump at the edge of the trees. 'There's always that.'

Catherine thinks about it no longer. She lifts her legs away from the pommels, sits side-on and jumps to the ground, twisting to face the mare as she does so.

'Bravo!' The girl claps her hands. Then, 'Are you all right, miss?' as Catherine sways, dizzy, and leans her head against Molly's flank.

'It's fine, I'm fine.'

'I don't think so. Are you feeling faint? Here, lean on me and we can use that stump as a seat.'

The girl is strong as promised. Catherine leans against her. They are of a height but the girl is fuller figured, easily able to support Catherine's thin body.

'Apple cider, that's what we need.' She feels Catherine's forehead where beads of sweat prickle. 'Good for dizziness. Or ginger tea. But for now ...' She gently pushes Catherine's head down. 'Stay here while I fetch water.'

Catherine grips the edge of the stump, willing the dizziness away. Nausea rises in her throat and she swallows it down. Even if she can remount, she worries she won't be able to stay in the saddle. Perhaps Papa is right, that she is not well enough to ride, not in this sticky warmth. His muted anger at her foolishness, his disappointment in her, worsens the discomfort curdling in her stomach.

A patterned clay mug of well water appears under her nose. She takes hold of it with shaking hands, sips. The coolness fizzes in her parched mouth like liquid sherbet, tingling on her tongue. She gulps the rest with the passion of a lost, thirst-tormented soul falling upon an oasis.

'It's silly,' she says, handing the mug to the girl. 'I get dizzy spells, my head feels heavy ...'

The girl lifts Catherine's chin and frowns into her eyes in the manner of Dr Newton. Catherine quashes a desire to laugh. She has no wish to insult her young nurse.

'Your eyes ...' The girl presses cool fingers to the sides of Catherine's face and gazes towards the beech and oak on the little valley's side. She murmurs in a clear, low voice. The unintelligible words echo from the trees in a silvery tinkle which puts Catherine in mind of muted windchimes.

The girl waits for perhaps a slow count of ten and removes her hands.

Catherine's dizziness flows away like the stream pours from the well through its arch before tumbling down moss-slippery steps to a marshy pond.

'Did that help?'

Catherine looks into the girl's warm eyes. 'It did.'

Her earlier notion that she is witnessing the young St Ceyna returns. The girl belongs in this place, attended by sprites as she draws from its waters, shade, and coolness to carry healing in her hands under the guidance of watchful souls.

She smiles softly. Fanciful ideas. Papa would tell her she should read fewer novels.

She cannot, however, deny the exquisite sensations rippling through her body. It's like lightning pulses through her veins. Her smile broadens.

The nausea is gone, the leaden state of her limbs is lifted. Her arms rise as if they would float away from her. She turns her hands palms up, fingers curling to scatter the sparkling specks of sunlight which swirl between her and the girl like a diaphanous veil. The air beneath the green canopy is luminous, and filled with susurrations of murmuring souls.

Life, they whisper, we bring life.

Catherine draws their whispers deep into her lungs, pushes her knuckles to her chest and greedily sucks in the promised life as if she is a newborn at its mother's breast.

The girl dangles the empty mug in one hand. The other hand is pressed to grinning lips. Her practical farmer's daughter air, her concerned nurse frown, have slid from her like a discarded cloak. She giggles.

The water sprites cavort about her, pearly wings flashing. They touch their tiny feet lightly to her face, her neck, her bare arms before springing back to ride the sunbeams eddying like gold-lit whirlpools.

'Imagine,' the girl says with teasing eyes. 'Imagine bathing with St Ceyna in her well. Imagine …'

Catherine imagines. And laughs a glittering laugh of joy.

Five days, five nights

One of my favourite places in the Forest is the sculpture near the bottom of Bixslade which commemorates the 1904 Union Pit disaster. Miners broke through into abandoned, water-filled tunnels, flooding their workings. Four men died, including two brothers whose deaths are memorialised in the sculpture.

HOW HIGH DID THE WATER rise? Did it lap at the toes of those who had found life-saving height on handy rocky shelves? Did it embrace waists, the cold fingers of a no-longer-desired lover tugging at drenched trousers? Or did it soak through heavy flannelled shirts to turn arms and shoulders into numbed sponges?

I'd followed the guide book's instructed way along an old 'dram' road which had once filled the narrow valley floor. Pocked, rectangular stones part-buried in the reddish clay and tufted grass confirmed my path. Beating aside nettles and brambles, I imagined away the overgrown greenery and pictured instead bare soil, scarred rocks, and gouges in the earth which turned to streaming rivulets after rain. If I listened hard on the still air, I was sure I would hear the ghosted cries of men and the heavy breaths of horses at their sweaty toil.

The dog nosed along behind, sniffing out long-buried odours.

At the end of the dram road, a plaque on a stone revealed the raw facts: water from abandoned mine workings flooding through the tunnels; seven men trapped; five days before rescuers reached them; four dead.

What did they speak of through their eternal black wait? Hope, surely – 'Don't give up, owld butt … summat'll happen, doan thee worry now.' Of hunger? Or did the exhaustion of keeping upright against the turgid sucking pull drive away hunger? Did they drink the greasy water, thickened like broth with dirt and coal dust? The water which was both life-giver and life-taker.

I closed my eyes against the bright sun, understanding I would never, even in the darkest reaches of a moonless, starless night, be able to simulate the black, wet horror of that flooded tunnel. I took a deep breath, shook my head and opened my eyes to look at the statue sitting above the plaque.

Two men, larger than life. Only their upper bodies are sculpted, legs buried in rock as cold and unforgiving as a shroud. It's a monument to death, and to a fierce compassion. One miner faces outwards, stolid, his eyes blank, his mouth downturned as he bears the weight of the other who clings to him. This one's head is thrown back in surrender to the flood. He's near death, and he's dragging his brother down — for I thought of them as the two brothers among those taken lifeless from the black waters. Thomas and Amos, their arms entwined and their hands clasped, both carried into forgetfulness by this new Lethe.

The dog, bored with the inaction, nudged my leg. I turned away, back to the dram road and my sunlit hike up the slade.

Cheryl Burman

AUSTRALIAN INSPIRED

Orchard kingdom

As very young children, we neighbourhood kids played in an old almond orchard, one of the last vestiges of rural life not yet fallen victim to rapidly spreading post WW2 suburbia. Nowadays, even the suburb of simple weatherboard homes which I remember has been swept away by glass and brick modernity.

Winner of the adult section of the 2020 Ottery St Mary writing competition. Also published in Dragon Gift, *2021.*

ONCE UPON A TIME, A leftover almond orchard lingered in our suburban street. The grown-ups walked by the orchard every day on their way to the bus or the train or the shops. Mostly they ignored it, although in spring their inward-looking eyes might stray outwards for a moment, to graze the pale pink petals fading to their magenta centre.

It was us children who knew the world which flourished among the twisted trunks of the almond trees. On hot summer mornings we escaped the dullard wizards and witches who would confine us to our weatherboard prisons. We slipped, one by one, two by two into the insect-buzzing grass between the trees. Provisioned with nectar of orange cordial, and slices of the softest bread filled with white and gold fragments of egg and carried in elf-made baskets of satiny tupperware, hunger could not call us away for hours at a time.

We children were kings and queens in our orchard kingdom. We stabbed holes with ragged fingernails into the stems of yellow flowers to weave crowns and royal necklaces. We built stone castles from fallen branches and dug moats of flattened grass. We jousted on stick chargers and brandished twiggy swords, clutched our ketchup bleeding hearts and roiled in deaths which left our hair and clothes covered in emerald seeds.

One day, a knight in golden bark armour scaled a tower tree to rescue a long-haired princess. He stretched to receive his silver-furred almond reward, and tumbled from his brave steed branch into the maw of the dragon roots below. The dragon took him, one piercing bite, and there the brave knight lay, pale and still.

The dullard wizards and witches wept, and forbad us kings and queens forever from the orchard kingdom. They imprisoned us in the weatherboard boxes and when the hundred years of our sentences had passed, we were sent into exile to the playground at the other end of the street.

The playground's hard wooden roundabout, molten metal slides and black asphalt surfaces scraped our bare knees and elbows, no longer protected by golden bark armour. We kings and queens rebelled, but when we scorned the hard-edged playground and sneaked to our orchard kingdom, we found our entry blocked.

Not by dragons, which we could have dealt with, but by a looming thicket of silver thorns adorned with spells warning Danger Keep Out in rampant red letters.

Worse, the thorny thicket wielded magic to conceal the orchard kingdom from our sight. No amount of squinting past the razor points would reveal our erstwhile country. The knobbled trees, the long grass and the yellow flowers had disappeared, hidden behind a veil of open hot sky and red earth scarred with trenches marked with lines of string.

The death of the Loch Ard

Originally written in response to a Twitter 7-day tale, where the prompt was 'It was a dark and stormy night', I have slightly expanded the story here.

Eighteen-year-old Eva Carmichael was one of two survivors of the wreck of the Loch Ard off the Australian coast in 1878. She clung to a spar for five hours in freezing waters, before being rescued by Tom Pearce, a young midshipman. And no, they didn't marry, despite spending time alone on a deserted beach with Eva in her night gown.

THE NIGHT IS DARK AS the inside of a whale's belly. Eva clings to her berth, heart thudding, her body tossed from side to side to match the frothing, roiling water hurling itself against the little ship.

The boom of the gale, the anguished groaning of the ship, the thunderous surges of water slapping onto the deck, meld with the terrified whimpered prayers of the passengers.

It seemed another life that Eva had been on deck, staring into the unremitting waves. Coldly green in the early days, turning indigo blue through the equator and now green again as they neared journey end. Always rearing up, falling back, like flexing muscles mocking the helpless ship and all her poor souls.

'Down below with you, miss.' The sailor had squinted at a sky darkened to a dusky violet. Chaotic clouds massed above the horizon.

Eva had obeyed, and at the urging of her mother prepared herself for bed. Used by now to the pitching and tossing, she had slept, intermittently. Now, in the darkest hours, she is frightenly awake. As is all the ship.

The berth pitches up, is vertical for a heartbeat, then plunges down with a violence which shakes loose Eva's fierce grip. The ship shudders. Her bones break in a shattering, squealing clamour.

The hatches surrender to the surging seas with a crashing bump. Icy waters gush through, filling the lower reaches of steerage like a kettle at a pump, drowning the crying children, drowning their praying, whimpering parents.

Just one more day and Eva would have been done forever with ships and waves. She will not be cheated, not now, after three months on the fragile heaving vessel. She clambers upright, wades through the chaos, grabbing at uprights still in place as she blindly searches for the ladder.

Water tosses her in its rage like a rag doll, but there...there are rungs. She clings, hauls herself upwards. Her sodden nightdress wraps itself shroud-like about her shivering body. She heaves, claws her way to the top, racing the rising seas.

She is out, lashed by rain and wind, crouched on all fours to lessen the impact of the gale. But she is alive, young, and strong. Dimly she is aware of sailors on the deck. They tug on ropes, desperation in every movement.

The ship lurches, slaps hard into the storming waves, and splits apart like kindling under an axe.

Eva grabs at a jagged-edged spar, its wet ropes flying in the wind. A crack like the call of doomsday. Eva and the spar tumble into the heaving, crashing green. Garbled prayers beat a rhythm in her head to match the terror in her soul …

AND THE REST

Carriers of grief

Highly commended 2021 Gloucestershire Writers Network Short Story competition on the theme Signposts. Readers of my novel Keepers *might recognise the bits I used for this tale set at a different time, in a different country.*

IT WAS ONLY THIS MORNING the boy from the post office panted up the hill on his bicycle. He pushed the envelope into Jean's hands, muttering, 'Telegram.' He didn't wait for a reply but bumped back down the stony track, wheels clattering in a tuneless accompaniment to the cawing of the magpie watching from the pine.

One for sorrow ...

The baby's yank at Jean's hem brings her wandering thoughts to heel. She stands on tiptoe, grunts, 'Ugh' and fights the chill gusts to lob the sodden sheet across the line. The effort thrusts her backwards, stumbling. The baby's fists flail at air and Jean snatches at his hand, saving him from a tumble down the nettle-covered slope. He wails his panic.

Jean scoops him up, presses his blond head against her shoulder. 'It's okay, Petey,' she murmurs. His wailing sinks to a hiccoughing sob. Jean sways, patting his back. She glances up. Above the pines lining the ridge, dirty clouds froth like scum in a copper. The sky has turned to buff, the clouds holding their own wet miseries.

Jean hasn't opened the telegram. Magpies notwithstanding, telegrams are carriers of grief. They spell 'final' in broken, hurried type. She fingered it for a moment before propping it against the bread crock while she tended a waking, crying Petey with all the emotion of a puppet.

Afterwards, while the water heated for the washing, she chose instead to read (again) Johnny's letter from Crete, where the sun shone in the May sky and the locals feted the Tommies as if each was Herakles reborn.

Jean pats the baby's back and slips into memory of another May sky.

A day off for both of them. Johnny had borrowed a bicycle, Jean had her own. They rode the country lanes through hedgerows flush with white blackthorn, purple violets and the yellow green of golden saxifrage.

'Which way?' Johnny asked at a crossroad where the wooden post had been stripped of its directive sign.

Jean pointed left. 'Good thing I'm local.' She'd laughed and he'd leaned his bicycle towards her, agreeing it was indeed, and too bad for any invading Germans. Jean flushed at his closeness, and at the remembered warmth of his lips on hers when they'd taken advantage of covert shadows behind the village hall as the residents welcomed the newly arrived soldiers.

Petey's cries turn to gurgles. Jean sets him on the grass. 'Stay there.' She hands him a wooden peg as an ersatz toy and strides back into battle. She unravels the sheet, pulling it taut against the moist flurries which hiss through the pines, insisting that all her efforts are worthless now.

Too soon, Johnny's blue eyes had smiled his farewells, his beret tipped at the required jaunty angle, uniform crisply in order. Handsome and knows it. She smiled her own come home farewell.

The grim morning darkens, the broiling clouds blacken. Squalling rain wets Jean's row of boiled nappies. The drops coalesce, fall faster, wind-whipped, harder, chillier. The sheet cracks like a lion tamer's whip.

'Damn, damn and damn!' she cries into the wind.

Petey grizzles. He lifts his face to the cold water and brandishes the inadequate peg above his quivering lips. Thunder rumbles. Petey's sobs gather fury. Jean dashes the wetness from her lashes and reaches for him, trying to throttle the sob snaking up her throat like an attacking soldier.

But as she leans to the baby, the sheet kicks out a sharp, wet edge. Smack! It catches her eye, stinging. Her tears break through this lapse in the defences and gather reinforcements in the streaming rain. She wraps her arms about her shrieking child and runs to the house, dumps him onto the porch, draws in a breath and returns, blind, into the tempest to rescue the laundry basket's sodden contents.

The magpie caws its defiance of the wind and the rain.

One for sorrow ...

Jean opens the telegram in the evening. After she has laid Petey in his cot and patted him to sleep, after she has brought her cocoa to the sagging couch, after she has set the mug on the floor and drawn her legs beneath her – after all that, she breathes deeply ... and does indeed find sorrow.

The clarity of sun on water

Carrying on the World War II theme, this story was inspired by a scene in Keepers. *It was longlisted in the 2021 Flash 500 Annual Short Story competition.*

JACK HAS CADGED THE LOAN of a jeep. The ruts in the road are hard as concrete and deep as trenches and the growling jeep judders and jerks like a fifth of November jumping jack. Elsie is crushed in the back, thigh to thigh with a dark-haired girl whose name she's forgotten. Ted acts as a bolster on one side while his crewcut mechanic friend offers the same service on the other. Or at least his legs do, as he's perched on the back clinging to the spare wheel. In the front, the dark-haired girl's room mate clutches rugs and the picnic basket to her chest and sways with the jeep. She'd elbowed the dark-haired girl aside, gloating as she settled in beside Jack who is, of course, driving. The gloating lips have thinned into a grim line but that hasn't lightened the dark-haired girl's surliness. In between jolts, Elsie sighs at this possible blight on her free day.

From time to time she grabs at her hat which is desperate to give in to the tugging wind despite its tied ribbons. She is constantly flung against Ted who has to press his shoulder into hers to save both of them from an ignominious sprawl into the dust. When the jeep takes flight over a mountainous bump, Elsie lurches into Ted's lap.

He eases her upright, ears pink. 'Careful there, Elsie.' He lets out a shrill giggle. 'Folks'll talk.'

Elsie gives him a quick glance before another bounce shoves her hard against the dark-haired girl.

'Can't he slow down? We've got all day.' The girl has found something else to be surly about.

'Nearly there,' Jack shouts, looking over his shoulder to check his passengers are still on board.

He winks at Elsie. She flushes, annoying herself, and flaps the hand not holding the hat. 'Eyes front, soldier,' she calls, unable to stop her flush deepening at the memory of last night's kiss. His lips warm on hers, taking advantage of the covert shadows of the shrubbery behind the nurses' block.

The jeep skews sideways in a drift of sand and Jack hauls on the big wheel. He accelerates through, shouting his victory over the vehicle and the sand.

The road ends at a headland. To either side and behind them the heathland is green and yellow with lumpy gorse, sharp-edged in the clear morning light. Ahead, the smooth sea glistens silver where it's touched by the spring sun. Gulls wheel and shriek, perhaps anticipating handouts, and so early in the year too. Elsie stands on unmoving ground, sucking the wind into her lungs, tasting salt and sunshine.

'Here, take this.' The surly girl shoves the basket into Elsie's hands. 'Don't dawdle, let's get onto the beach.'

The path winds down to a sunlit calm. The room mate spreads the rugs on dry sand between rocks and Elsie sets the basket in the middle but doesn't open it. It's too early to eat. Besides, the wild drive, the windy clifftop, the hustling gulls, have stirred their blood and no one can stay still.

'Let's walk to the headland.' The mechanic waves to where the cove ends in a curve of gunmetal grey rocks and sheer umber cliffs. A small lighthouse surveys the sea for potential wrecks. Elsie imagines its white light cutting the night to save the lives of imperilled sailors. Like the white lights which cut the night sky above London, except the London lights herald death to those they reach.

They wander the yellow beach under a sun which heats Elsie's cheeks despite her hat. She ties her cardigan around her waist, rolls up the wide legs of her trousers, and gives her shoes into Ted's outstretched hands. He stays out of reach of the waves, watching over Elsie as she paddles in the lacy froth of the shallows. A soft breeze gently promises summer.

'Almost warm enough to swim,' she says to the air. 'If you're brave enough.'

Jack is the only one not to laugh.

'Plenty warm enough,' he says. 'I'm going in.'

He pulls off his khaki trousers to reveal red bathing trunks which flatter his olive-skinned slim legs. His tie and jacket have already been abandoned to the picnic rugs, so he only has his shirt to remove. A hairless chest, well-muscled, Elsie sees before turning away. She keeps her eyes on the glittering blue water, chiding herself for her foolishness. After all, she's seen any number of chests, hairless or hairy, always muscled, these past two years.

'Coming?' Jack challenges Ted.

'No thanks. Too cold for me.' Ted hugs his arms around his body and shivers.

'What about you, bud?'

The mechanic snorts. 'Might be sharks.'

'This ain't Florida,' Ted says. 'Too cold for sharks.'

'Call yourself soldiers?' Jack shrugs hugely, smirks at Elsie and runs towards the sea. He waves an arm in farewell, lifting the scars which streak like pink lightning across his back.

The tide is out and he splashes a long way, arms flailing, legs kicking up shimmering sprays before he dives into the water. His dark head emerges, seal-like, then one arm and another. He swims on, in the direction he was running, towards the horizon.

They all watch.

'Is he going to swim home to the good ol' US of A?' the surly girl mutters.

'Going in the wrong direction,' Elsie says. She chews her lip. 'Could end up in France though.'

Ted shakes his head. 'Last place he'd want to go back to.'

Jack keeps swimming, a black dot against the silver water.

The room mate shades her eyes from the glare. 'He should be heading back.' She makes it sound proprietary. The surly girl sniffs.

Elsie thinks Jack should be heading back too.

'Silly bugger.' Ted shakes his head. 'Hope there're no currents out there.'

No one knows about currents. Jack swims on.

'Heading off into the blue, just like that.' Ted snaps his fingers. 'Does what he likes, no thought for what might happen, who's gonna worry.'

'Should we do something?' The room mate chews on a fingernail and casts quick looks between Ted and the tiny figure out in the water.

'No.' The surly girl flutters an arm in Jack's direction. 'See, he's stopped.'

Elsie squints. Jack has indeed stopped. Is he resting? Or in trouble?

'Come on,' the surly girl urges. 'Let's walk along the beach, pretend we never saw him.' She humphs. 'Pathetic, showing off like a stupid kid. He needs to grow up.'

She tosses her room mate a triumphant look, vindicated somehow, and marches towards the headland with long impatient strides.

The room mate shakes her head and darts forward to link her arm in the mechanic's, smiling into his surprised face. He grins, and they stroll the sand, heads down searching for shells.

Elsie stays where she is, her hand to her forehead, gaze fixed on the water. Someone needs to make sure Jack isn't in trouble. Ah! Here he comes, swimming, slowly, to the shore.

'He'll be all right.' Ted stands a little way ahead, calling to Elsie. 'He won't drown. Jack's a lucky bastard.'

Elsie glances at him, and back to the water.

Ted's feet are poised to follow the others, his diffident stance competing with the coaxing tilt of his head.

'Coming?' he says, lifting his chin.

Elsie kicks at the gritty sand. She's angry at herself for letting Jack's silly antics trouble her. What's Jack to her? She shouldn't think about him. Better to think about kind and considerate Ted.

She shrugs her shoulders high, waves at Ted and laughs.

'Coming,' she calls, and turns her back on the sea.

Guy Fawkes, guy, 'twas his intent to blow up king and parliament

Written in response to a writing prompt at a workshop. In the UK, Bonfire Night is marked with fires and fireworks each year on 5th November to celebrate the foiling of a plot to blow up the Houses of Parliament on that date in 1605. One of the key ringleaders was Guido (Guy) Fawkes. For centuries, a straw dummy of Fawkes – known as a guy – would be made and burned on bonfires.

THE DAY – THE NIGHT – IS HERE.

The children hold their guys high, lovingly made ready for this moment over the last days. Their creators raided their mothers' store rooms for rags, begged trousers and shirts from willing fathers, and competed with each other for who has painted the most expressive face or whose guy is the best dressed. As each was finished, it was bound to a pole and carried through the village, its proud owner begging for a penny for some noble cause.

The children laugh and jiggle, guys bobbing, excitement bubbling.

The mayor, magnificent in gilded chain and scarlet robes, takes up a flaming torch and thrusts it deep into the great bonfire.

Day by day the children watched the bonfire grow on the village green. The moment school was out they were there, measuring the progress since yesterday. Men and women toiled to steadily build the familiar shape, taller and taller. They scooped great armfuls of furze and brush culled from the forest and set it in place, layer upon layer. Long leafless branches, left to dry in barns and sheds all year, were delivered to the green in farmers' wagons and piled all around like a sloping stockade.

The villagers cheer as the flames leap, devouring the furze, the brush, turning the dried out branches to glowing rods of gold and red to outshine the mayor's effulgent costume.

Parents and teachers have told the story over and over: the planning and plotting, the secrets which had to be kept close, the names of those who had to be bribed and those who joined willingly. They told about the rain filling the filthy puddles of London that chill night, the soft-footed creeping through the lightless passages, capture and torture possible at every turn, the setting of the fuses …

The children never tire of hearing that tale of the first fifth of November.

They parade with their guys, around and around the fiery heap, laughing and chanting – Remember, remember, the fifth of November. The grownups weave among them, singing – Guy Fawkes, guy, t'was his intent, To blow up king and parliament – and cheer again when the flimsy copy of the old parliament building roars into flame, burning, burning, before collapsing into the coals with a whump!

The people dance in the firelight glow and give thanks to that first Guy – the valiant man who saved them all those years ago from the venal corruption of parliament and the sinful waste of monarchy.

Peacock kite

This piece of flash fiction came 3rd in the 2022 Ottery St Mary writing competition with its theme Trapped.

THE BOY IS TOO SMALL. The kite too big.

Blustering squalls which whip the grasses sloping to the cliff edge tumble the kite through a louring evening sky like a nest-less fledgling. Its ribboned tail tangles in a snarl of colours. The boy clings to the line, arms tight against its drag. His head bobs, keeping time with his flying toy.

I squint into the wind. Where is the father who this morning laughed with this boy on the sunny beach, guiding his small hands on the line?

Petrichor had hung in the air, as much proof of the passed shower as the glistering drops which turned the sea thrift to pink tourmaline. I had stooped to gather the rosette-hearted flowers, curious if their semblance to the jewel might keep the devils in their hells. For a time.

Roused by a child's joyous shriek, I lifted my head to find the father, son, and the glorious kite. Peacock-shaped, brilliant wings outstretched, its tail feathers coursed across a fresh-washed sky.

Turning back to my gathering, my hand hovered over the tempting yellow poison of horned poppy. No. I touched a finger to my 'tourmaline' and snipped grey fronds of wormwood. Healing fronds, pressed to cuts and bruises. Should they be called for.

The boy had run along the sand, the kite filling his world. The father proffered me a quick glance and strode away without so much as touch to his hat.

Now, on the cliff top, a tumultuous wind eddies around the kite, tosses it higher, still higher. The kite surges, falls, gorging on the gusts to soar above the white-capped waves thundering against the rocks below. Gulls rise from their nests, screeching reproof.

The boy's eyes are fixed on the kite. His feet in their shiny leather boots slither on wet grass, legs taut, body unbalanced. The peacock wings swallow the turbulence, swelling and collapsing in imitation of the billowing waves. They yank the boy, tugging, hauling him towards the gulls – towards the plummeting drop.

Four more stumbling steps. Three. Two …

Let go! I scream against the wind. Let go!

He cannot let go, cannot escape the kite's unrelenting drag. The boy is as ensnared as a fish on a worm-laden hook.

No time to ponder, to consider the consequences of confirmation.

I spread my arms, body lifting … and I am flying … fighting the storm … arms braced, fingers clawed to pluck and save …

Acknowledgements

My thanks to those who have contributed to these stories in various ways, either by introducing me to a piece of history, critiquing the stories, or offering a competition which inspired me to write.

And as ever, my special thanks to my husband David Harris for his design and production work.

Cheryl Burman grew up as the child forever reading on her bed. But as this was Australia, she was also often tempted outside to the beach and the yabby creeks near her suburban home. When she moved to the Forest of Dean, UK, she followed the likes of Tolkien, Rowling and many others in being inspired to write. As a devout Narnia fan, she started with middle grade fantasy, discovered a taste for historical fiction, and then combined the two into historical fantasy.

Given she is lucky enough to live in a place chock-a-block full of history, legend and myth, there is much to draw on. She does so, as well as on her own childhood in Australia.

Two of her novels have won awards, as have several of her flash fiction pieces and short stories. Some of these are included in her two short story collections, while others are published in various anthologies.

A keen student of writing craft, Cheryl has had articles published on writing-related topics both online and in print, and maintains a popular writing tips post on her blog.

As Cheryl Mayo, she is a former chair of Dean Writers Circle and a founder of Dean Scribblers, which encourages creative writing among young people in her community.

Find her and her books at https://cherylburman.com/
Follow her on twitter @cr_burman and on
Facebook at https://www.facebook.com/CherylBurmanAuthor

Printed in Great Britain
by Amazon